D1505627

IT'S NOT ABOUT THE
STRAW!

Veronika Martenova Charles

Illustrated by David Parkins

TUNDRA BOOKS

Text copyright © 2013 by Veronika Martenova Charles
Illustrations copyright © 2013 by David Parkins

Published in Canada by Tundra Books, a division of Random House of Canada Limited,
One Toronto Street, Suite 300, Toronto, Ontario M5C 2V6

Published in the United States by Tundra Books of Northern New York,
P.O. Box 1030, Plattsburgh, New York 12901

Library of Congress Control Number: 2012945435

Library and Archives Canada Cataloguing in Publication

Charles, Veronika Martenova
      It's not about the straw! / Veronika Martenova Charles ; illustrated
by David Parkins.

(Easy-to-read wonder tales)
Short stories based on Rumpelstiltskin tales from around the world.
ISBN 978-1-77049-326-1. – ISBN 978-1-77049-331-5 (EPUB)

      1. Fairy tales. I. Parkins, David II. Title. III. Series: Charles,
Veronika Martenova. Easy-to-read wonder tales.

PS8555.H4224211838 2013   jC813'.54   C2012-905310-4

We acknowledge the financial support of the Government of Canada through the
Canada Book Fund and that of the Government of Ontario through the Ontario Media
Development Corporation's Ontario Book Initiative. We further acknowledge the support of
the Canada Council for the Arts and the Ontario Arts Council for our publishing program.

ONTARIO ARTS COUNCIL
CONSEIL DES ARTS DE L'ONTARIO

Edited by Stacey Roderick

www.tundrabooks.com

Printed and bound in China

1 2 3 4 5 6   18 17 16 15 14 13

CONTENTS

ON THE FARM
PART 1

On Sunday, Lily, Ben, and Jake

went to visit Jake's grandmother

on her farm.

"I'll make some lunch for you.

I'll call you when it's ready,"

said Jake's grandma.

"Let's go outside to explore,"

Jake said to Lily and Ben.

They went to see

the chickens and the rabbits.

Then they walked into the barn.

"Look at all the straw!" said Ben.

"If we could turn it into gold,

we would be rich!"

"That's true," said Jake.

"But we'd need that little man

to help us, like in the story.

And we would have to

guess his name."

"What's his name?" asked Ben.

"Rum-pel-stilt-skin," replied Jake.

"I know another story,

but the little man has

a different name," said Lily.

"And it's not about the straw."

"What is it about?" asked Ben.

"I'll tell you," replied Lily.

ELF

(Rumpelstiltskin from Germany)

In the woods behind a village

there were big rocks.

Inside them, in a cave,

lived an elf.

He often came to the village

dressed only in his underpants.

This annoyed people.

Otherwise, he didn't get

in anybody's way.

One day, a girl named Elsa

was picking berries in the woods.

She slipped on the rocks,

fell in between two boulders,

and couldn't get out.

"Help!" she screamed.

The elf heard her and came.

"Please," said Elsa,

"can you pull me out of here?

I will sew some nice clothes

for you to wear."

"I will only help you,"

replied the elf,

"if you come back every day

and try to guess my name.

If, by the third day,

you don't get it right,

you have to marry me."

Elsa thought, *Guessing his name*

shouldn't be that hard.

And if he doesn't help me,

I'll die from hunger and cold.

"I'll do as you ask," Elsa promised.

So the elf rescued her.

The elf was waiting

when Elsa came back the next day.

"Is your name Andy?" Elsa asked.

"Could it be Bert? Edwin? Freddy?

Harry? Jay? Rupert? Waldo?"

"Not even close," laughed the elf.

"See you tomorrow."

Elsa began to worry.

Perhaps his name is not ordinary,

she thought.

So, on the second day,

Elsa guessed differently:

"Is your name Elm? Spruce?

Fir? Woodsy? Sandy? Rocky?"

"I haven't got all day,"

said the elf.

"Tomorrow is your last chance."

And he hopped inside his cave.

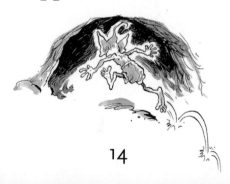

Elsa went home very upset.

If she didn't guess the elf's name,

she would have to marry him.

Just then, the neighbor's boy

walked by and saw Elsa

sitting on the porch, crying.

"What's the matter?" the boy asked.

"I'll tell you something funny

to cheer you up," he said.

"I was walking in the woods,"

said the boy.

"Near the rocks,

I lay down to have a nap.

I heard someone singing,

It's so great she doesn't know

that my name is Hop-and-Go!

I peeked between the rocks

and saw an elf clapping his hands

and hopping around like crazy!"

"Thank you for telling me!"

exclaimed Elsa.

She gave the boy a big hug.

Elsa stayed up through the night

sewing a nice jacket and pants

for the elf to wear

so she could give him something

for rescuing her.

The next morning, Elsa went

to the woods without fear.

"Your last guess?" asked the elf.

Elsa placed the jacket and pants

in front of the elf.

"These are for you, Hop-and-Go!"

"Aaarrgh!" screeched the elf.

Then he took the clothes

and hopped over the rock.

And that was the last time

anyone saw him.

"You know what's funny?"

asked Jake.

"One of the names Elsa said

is my middle name."

"Which one?" asked Lily.

"I'll tell you later," said Jake.

"First, I'll tell you another story

about guessing a name."

"Is it about an elf, too?" asked Lily.

"No," replied Jake.

"It's about an evil fairy!"

LADY IN GREEN

(*Rumpelstiltskin* from Scotland)

Jack lived with his mother

in a cottage on a hill.

They were poor

but had a pet pig

they called Gracie.

Every morning,

Jack fed Gracie in the barn.

Then he played and ran with her,

up and down the hill.

One day, Jack found the pig

in the barn, shivering.

"What's the matter with her?"

he asked his mother.

"Gracie must be sick," she said.

They covered Gracie with a blanket

and brought her favorite food.

"I hope she gets better soon,"

said Mother.

But Gracie didn't.

She stayed in the barn,

didn't eat, and didn't move.

"Mother, is Gracie going to die?"

asked Jack.

"I don't know, Son," she replied.

Later, they saw a lady in green

coming up the road.

Jack's mother stood to greet her.

"Why are you so sad?"

the lady asked.

"Our pig is sick and may be dying,"

she answered.

"What will you give me

if I cure your pig?" asked the lady.

"Anything you'd like,"

Jack's mother replied.

"It's a deal, then," said the lady,

and she went into the barn.

She took out of her pocket

a tiny bottle of green oil

and rubbed it on Gracie's snout.

Then she muttered something.

Finally, she said, "Get up, beast!"

As soon as she said it,

Gracie stood up

and went to eat her food.

Jack's mother was so happy,

she bent down to kiss

the hem of the lady's dress.

31

"Stop that," said the lady.

"Let's settle our bargain.

All I ask, and *will have*, is your son."

Jack's mother, who knew now

she was dealing with a fairy,

started to wail.

"Your crying won't help you,"

said the lady in green.

"But I can tell you this:

By our fairy law, I can't

claim your son until the third day.

And not even then

if you can guess my name."

Then she turned around and left.

Jack's mother couldn't sleep.

She wrote down all the names

she could think of,

but she knew the fairy's name

probably wouldn't be common.

On the second day,

as Jack was playing outside,

Gracie suddenly took off

and ran toward the woods.

Jack chased her

to bring her back.

Gracie jumped over fallen trees

and stopped at the edge of a cliff.

Jack caught up with Gracie

and looked down over the ledge.

There, dancing by the stream,

was the lady in green, singing,

Tomorrow is the day

when the child I want, I will claim,

'cause nobody can guess

that Allegra is my name.

Jack ran back home with Gracie

and told his mother

what he had seen and heard.

She was so happy!

She wrote down the name Allegra

so as not to forget it.

On the third day,

the lady in green came back.

"So," she said, "what's my name?"

Jack's mother pretended to think.

"Give me your son right now!"

ordered the lady.

"Please," said the mother,

"take me instead,

mighty fairy Allegra!"

The lady in green spun around

and backed down the hill,

never to be seen again.

"So, what is your middle name?"

Lily asked Jake.

"Wait!" interrupted Ben.

"Now it's my turn to tell a story

about guessing a name.

Only it's about an ogre ..."

THE BRIDGE

(*Rumpelstiltskin* from Japan)

Ever since Shiro was a boy,

he liked to build things

out of sticks and stones.

"When I grow up,"

he told his father,

"I want to be a great builder."

Shiro studied hard, and in time

he became the most famous builder

in the land.

One day,

two men came to see him.

"Our village sits on the banks

of a big, wide river," they said.

"Twice we built a bridge,

but the river washed both away.

Could you build a bridge for us?"

Shiro agreed

and travelled to their village.

Never in his life had Shiro seen

a river so wild.

It would be hard to build a bridge

that would stand up to the current.

As he was thinking about it,

a horrible ogre rose from the river.

"What are you doing here?"

the ogre asked.

"I came to build a bridge,"

Shiro replied.

"No human can build a bridge
strong enough to stand up
to this river," said the ogre.
"But *I* can build it for you
if you'll pay my price."
Shiro agreed.

He spent the night in a local inn.

In the morning, Shiro returned.

He couldn't believe his eyes!

A strong, splendid bridge

arched high above the raging river.

Not even in the rainy season

could water reach that high.

As Shiro gazed in wonder

at the bridge,

the ogre broke through the water.

"So," the ogre roared,

"let's settle the price.

I want you to give me your eyes."

"My eyes!" Shiro shivered.

"But how can I?" he asked.

"If I give you my eyes,

I won't be able to do my work!"

Shiro fell to his knees

and pleaded with the ogre.

"Pitiful creature!" said the ogre.

"I'll give you one chance

to get out of our deal.

If, by sunset, you guess my name,

you can keep your eyes.

If not, I'll come after you,

take your eyes, and kill you."

Then the ogre dove

under the water.

Shiro trembled in terror.

Shiro went into the forest

and tried to decide what to do.

As he walked deeper and deeper,

he heard some voices.

He went closer

and peeked through the trees.

In the clearing, he saw children

with horns on their heads

dancing and singing.

Sixth Ogre Oniroku never lies;

he promised to bring human eyes.

Oniroku will bring us a treat;

human eyes, that's what we'll eat!

"Sixth Ogre Oniroku,"

Shiro whispered to himself.

"That must be the ogre's name!

And these must be his children!"

He hurried back to the river.

The sun was setting.

Just then, the ogre

burst through the water.

"So," he roared,

"can you guess my name?

You can try three times."

Shiro pretended to think.

"Is your name

Red Ogre Akaoni?" he asked.

"No, it's not," laughed the ogre.

"Then could it be

Eighth Ogre Onihachi?"

This time, the ogre turned pale.

"No," said the ogre.

"You might as well give up.

Give me your eyes!"

And the ogre stretched

his hairy arm toward Shiro.

"Wait!" called Shiro.

"I still have one more try.

Your name is Sixth Ogre Oniroku!"

At that moment,

the ogre sank beneath the river.

Only giant bubbles remained.

Shiro was relieved.

He returned home.

The bridge that the ogre built

was never destroyed by the river,

even after a heavy rain.

★ ★ ★

ON THE FARM
PART 2

"If Oniroku was the sixth ogre,"

said Jake,

"where were the others?"

"I think they lived in

different rivers," Ben replied.

"Jake," said Lily,

"tell us your middle name now."

"You have to guess!" said Jake.

"What will we get

if we guess right?" asked Lily.

"Well," said Jake,

"if Grandma made an apple pie,

I'll give you an extra piece."

"It's a deal," said Lily.

"Is your middle name Andy?"
she asked.

"No, it's not," replied Jake.

"Is it Waldo or Harry?" asked Ben.

"Wrong again," said Jake.

"What about Edwin?" asked Lily.

"You guessed it!" said Jake.

"Well, you said it was a name
from the story I told," Lily replied.

Just then, the barn door opened,
and Jake's grandma came in.

"I've been calling you.

Lunch is ready," she said.

"What's for dessert?" Jake asked.

"Apple pie," Grandma replied.

"You're in luck!"

Jake told Lily and Ben,

and they ran to the farmhouse.

★

ABOUT THE STORIES

Rumpelstiltskin, a fairy tale collected and set in print by the Grimm brothers in 1812, is the most popular of the stories about guessing a name. There are similar stories in different cultures, and the ones collected here are three examples.

Elf is inspired by a tale from Germany called *Kugerl,* first recorded in 1854, and is one of many versions of *Rumpelstiltskin* found there.

Lady in Green is based on a story called *Whuppity Stoorie* from Scotland.

The Bridge is a retelling of a Japanese tale called *Carpenter and Oniroku.*